The new baby

For Henry

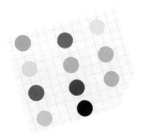

First published in the United Kingdom in 2018 by
Pavilion Children's Books
43 Great Ormond Street
London
WC1N 3HZ

An imprint of Pavilion Books Company Limited

ISBN: 9781843653561

A CIP catalogue record for this book is available from the British Library.

10 9 8 7 6 5 4 3 2 1

Reproduction by Mission, Hong Kong
Printed by Toppan Leefung Printing Ltd,China
Designed by Lee-May Lim

This book can be ordered directly from the publish
www.pavilionbooks.com, or try your local bookshop

The new baby

by lisa stickley

PAVILION

My name is Edith. I am little.

I am bigger than I was last year,
but not as big as I will be next year.

I have a new brother.
We call him Albert.

This is the story of our
first year together.

Albert arrived in January.

He arrived in a basket.

He was very small and covered in a flowery blanket.

He didn't do much, but we all knew when he was hungry.

An enormous Waaaaaaaa Waaaaaaaa Waaaaaaaaaaaa noise could be heard throughout the house.

I had to hold my ears.

Sometimes when everything was quiet...

...he would do teeny windy pops!

Phhhffffff

In February, mummy made
a mobile out of cardboard.

I helped.

Albert loved to look at it
from his cot.

I twirled it round and round.

Twiddle flutter twiddle flutter twiddly flutter.

Albert giggled.

In March, Albert befriended Gerald Giraffe.
Gerald rattles. Albert loves him.

Jingle jingle jingle boink
jingle jingle boink!

Albert often bumped Gerald on the floor. The poor giraffe got a sore head. I looked after him and gave him a plaster.

By April Albert's bottom was getting louder and the nappies were quite pongy. Sometimes noises could be heard from inside the pram when we were walking in the park.

Squelchy pooooop pop!

When he did a really smelly
one I had to hold my nose!

Poooooeeeeee!

In May, Albert was full of dribble.
He made LOTS of slurpy sloppy
sounds and blew raspberries...

PHLHLHLHLHuuuuuhhhh!

I tickled his toes. It made him laugh LOTS!

Squawk giggle tickle
tickle, squawk
giggle iggle iggle

He would giggle so much that I got COVERED
in slobbery raspberry spray. YUCK!

June was the month for sitting-up practice.
Albert got quite good but still flopped over a bit.
It was funny.

He would sit up perfectly in a pile of cushions.
Then very, very slowly he would lean to one side and...

WOOOOOOOOOOOOp

...go FLUMP in a heap!

By July, little Albert could peep over the edge of the bath.
Splash splosh giggle SPLOSH!
were the noises I made from behind the curtain.

Albert would laugh and laugh
when I peeked round and said

boo!

August was a messy month. Mummy started
feeding Albert funny mushed-up stuff.

SPLAT
splatter
fling slosh.

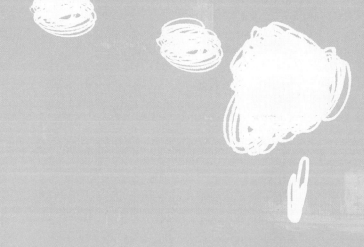

One day Albert flicked his spoon
and messy, gooey baby-food slop
splatted in a great big blob all
over the kitchen wall.

Then slowly it came
unstuck and went

plop

on the floor.

Albert had his first go on the swings in September.
It was great fun. I sat in the swing next to him.
Because he is so little Albert had a very gentle go.

whee swoosh whee swoosh

I am bigger and went really high!

WHIZZ WHOOSH WHIZZ
WHOOOOOOOOSSSSSSHHHHH!

I almost touched a cloud with my foot!

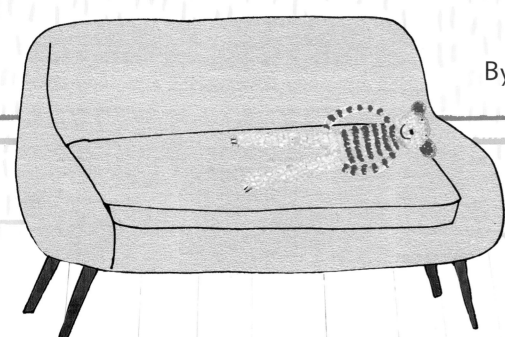

By October Albert was crawling fast!

But he didn't always look
where he was going.

Stamp stomp stomp boink
stomp stomp boink!

he went, as he head-butted the sofa.

Our favourite November game was tower building.
I would build a tower out of NINE cups.

Then Albert would power across the room
with a crawl like lightning, and with a
doink and a whack the tower
would fall to the ground

with an almighty

CRASH!

In December,
a wibbly-wobbly
Albert started
walking.

It was good that his nappy
was SO BIG and padded.

It saved him from bumps
and bruises as he wobbled
his way around...

Wibble wobble flump wibble wobble flump

Today we are having cake. Albert is a whole year old!

I help Albert to blow out his candle...

Phhhffffff

He can't quite do it yet.

In fact his puff sounds
a bit like his first ever
windy pop!

I love my little brother and
his funny noises.

Happy birthday Albert!